This one is for George, with love
Bernette Ford

For Archie and Dylan
love from Sam Williams

First American edition published in 2008
by Boxer Books Limited.

Distributed in the United States and Canada by
Sterling Publishing Co., Inc.
387 Park Avenue South, New York, NY 10016-8810

First published in Great Britain in 2008
by Boxer Books Limited.
www.boxerbooks.com

ISBN-13: 978-1-905417-89-6
ISBN-10: 1-905417-89-6

1 3 5 7 9 10 8 6 4 2

Printed in China

All of our papers are sourced from managed forests and renewable resources.

No More Pacifier for Piggy!

Bernette Ford and Sam Williams

Boxer Books

Piggy knocks on Ducky's door.

He is sucking on his pacifier.

Ducky peeks out the window.

"Peek-a-boo, Piggy!" she says.

"Do you want to play

a new game with me?"

Piggy nods his head up and down.

He tries to smile at Ducky,

but his pacifier is in the way.

Ducky and Piggy run out to the garden.

Piggy giggles . . .

and drops his pacifier on the ground.

"You can't have that now,"

says Ducky, "it's dirty!"

Piggy has another pacifier

in his pocket.

He pops it into his mouth.

Now Ducky hides behind her hands.

"Peek-a-boo, Piggy!" Ducky shouts.

"Peek-a-boo! I see you!"

Piggy tries to smile at Ducky.

But his pacifier is in the way.

Ducky hides behind a tree.

She peeks around it.

"Peek-a-boo, Piggy," calls Ducky.

"Peek-a-boo, I see you!"

Piggy laughs . . .

and drops his pacifier on the ground!

He looks in his pocket for another.

But he doesn't have one.

Piggy starts to cry.

He points to his pacifier in the dirt.

"What's the matter, Piggy?" asks Ducky.

"Don't you want to play with me?"

Piggy nods his head up and down.

Ducky picks up Piggy's pacifier

and puts it on the table.

"You're missing all the fun," she says.

"Come on, it's your turn now!"

So Piggy hides behind a lawn chair.

"Peek-a-boo, Ducky!" Piggy says softly.

"Peek-a-boo, I see you!"

Ducky laughs!

Piggy hides under the table.

"Peek-a-boo, Ducky!" he calls louder.

"Peek-a-boo, I see you!"

Ducky laughs again.

The two friends play together for hours,

and Piggy forgets all about his pacifier.

"Did you have fun today?" asks Ducky.

"Yes, I did!" Piggy shouts.

"No more pacifier for Piggy!"